princess natasha

student · secret agent · princess

PRINCESS NATASHA

student · secret agent · princess

#6 Sweet Nothings

Text by Stephanie Peters
Created by Larry Schwarz

Visit Princess Natasha every day at
www.princessnatasha.com.

Watch Princess Natasha anytime online
on the KOL® service at KW: Princess Natasha.

LITTLE, BROWN & COMPANY
LB kids™
NEW YORK BOSTON
lb-kids.com

Little, Brown and Company

Hachette Book Group USA
1271 Avenue of the Americas, New York, NY 10020
Visit our Web site at www.lb-kids.com

LB kids is an imprint of Little, Brown and Company Books for Young Readers, a division of Hachette Book Group USA.
The logo design and name, LB kids, are trademarks of Hachette Book Group USA.

First Edition: February 2007

The characters and events portrayed in this book are fictitious. Any similarity to real persons, living or dead, is coincidental and not intended by the author.

Based on the KOL® cartoon created by Animation Collective, Inc.

Library of Congress Cataloging-in-Publication Data

Peters, Stephanie True, 1965-
  Sweet nothings / text by Stephanie Peters ; created by Larry Schwarz; [illustrations by Animation Collective]. — 1st ed.
    p. cm.— (Princess Natasha ; #6)
  "Based on the KOL cartoon created by Animation Collective."
  ISBN-13: 978-0-316-15511-3
  ISBN-10: 0-316-15511-X
  I. Schwarz, Laurence. II. Animation Collective. III. Title. IV. Series:
Peters, Stephanie True, 1965-   . Princess Natasha ; #6.
PZ7.P441833Svw 2007
[Fic]—dc22

                                                        2006009926

10 9 8 7 6 5 4 3 2 1

COM-MO

Printed in the United States of America

Deep in the Carpathian Mountains lies the ancient kingdom of Zoravia. Usually, the people of this country live in peace and harmony. But there are times when darkness falls across this fair land—a darkness known as Lubek.

Fifteen years earlier, Lubek inherited control of Zoravia. But the people had long despised Lubek. They voted him off the throne and elected his brother, Carl, in his place.

Lubek fled to America and began scheming against his former homeland. For years, his exact whereabouts remained a mystery. Then Zoravian Intelligence discovered his secret identity. By day, Lubek works as a high school principal and science teacher in a small town in Illinois called . . . Zoravia.

Once known as Fountain Park, the town changed its name in honor of King Carl, Queen Lena, and their fourteen-year-old daughter, Princess Natasha. Natasha had never met her evil uncle, but she had spent her life preparing to defeat him.

And now, she'll have her chance. Trained as a secret agent, Natasha has come to Illinois, where she poses as an exchange student at Fountain Park High. No one—not her host family, her friend Maya, or her fellow students—can ever know her true identity. If Lubek ever found out who she was, it would be the end of Natasha—and her beloved Zoravia.

Chapter One

Video Mania

Thud! Thud! Thud!

Natasha—princess of Zoravia, foreign exchange student, and undercover secret agent—dropped her book and jumped. Someone was pounding on her bedroom door.

THUD! THUD! THUD!

"Okay, okay!"

She opened the door just as Greg O'Brien, the handsome teenage son of her host parents, kicked at it again. His foot connected with her shin instead.

"Ow!" Natasha cried. "What are you *doing*?"

Greg, his arms loaded with electronic equipment, elbowed her aside. "I need your room  to make my Valentine's Day present for Kelly."

Kelly was Greg's girlfriend. Girl*fiend* was a better term for her, in Natasha's opinion.

"Why my room?"

"It's got the best acoustics in the house. I'm making her a music video!" He picked up a microphone from the pile of gear, flung his head back, and opened his mouth in imitation of a rock star bellowing out a song.

"Well, that certainly will be special," Natasha said. She eyed the electric keyboard, video

 camera, and tripod. "Where'd you get all the equipment?"

"Mr. Lubek let me borrow it from the school."

Natasha's jaw dropped. "Mr. *Lubek*? You're kidding!"

"Yeah, he was pretty nice about it."

Natasha sat on her bed in shock. Lubek . . . *nice*?

Greg plugged in the keyboard and cranked the volume to high. "Listen to the song I made up." He began thumping his forefingers on the middle two piano keys.

Natasha recognized the tune immediately. "You're playing 'Chopsticks.'"

"No, I'm playing a keyboard."

He sang along with the music.

"Kel-ly, la la la la. Kel-ly, tra la la la. Kel-ly, blah blah blah blah. Kel-ly—"

"You've got an alert!"

A muffled voice, which seemed to come from the bedside table, interrupted Greg's song. He looked at her in puzzlement. "What'd you say?"

"What'd I say?" Natasha thought fast. "I said, you forgot a shirt!"

"You've got an alert!"

"See? I said it again!" She yanked Greg across the room and shoved him toward the door. "If you're going to make a music video, you have to dress like a rock star, right? So go change."

She pushed him out of the room and slammed the door in his face. Then she hurried to her bedside table and pulled out her Booferberry, the small telecommunicator that allowed her to keep in touch with her father, King Carl. His troubled face appeared on the screen.

"Dad! What's going on? You look worried."

The king sighed. "It's what's *not* going on that has me worried. Lubek has been quiet lately. *Too* quiet."

"He's been nice, too." Natasha told him how Lubek had helped Greg.

Her father looked grave. "I don't like it. Can you see what he's up to?"

"I'll put him under surveillance tonight," she promised.

Thud! Thud! Thud!

Natasha groaned. "I gotta go, Dad. Give Mom my love, okay? Natasha out."

She stowed away the Booferberry. Then she

opened her door, took one look at what was on the other side, and threw up her arms in mock horror. "Ahhh! My eyes!"

Greg was wearing a sequined vest over a tie-dyed T-shirt with gold harem pants. His hair had gone from sandy waves to jet-black spikes. Glittery eye shadow sparkled on his lids, and on his cheek was a badly drawn barbed-wire heart with "Kelly" written inside it.

"I decided to go for the goth-glam-grunge look," he said. "What do you think?" He took a step forward and tripped.

"I think you better not try to sing and dance at the same time." She helped him to his feet and then grabbed the video camera. "Now come on, Britney, let's get this video started!"

Chapter Two

A Thorny Situation

Two hours and one painful music video later, Natasha was crouched high atop the roof of a store, whispering into her Booferberry to her spy partner, Oleg Boynski.

"I've got a visual on Lubek and am in pursuit. Back in five."

She pocketed the tele-communicator and sprinted the length of the rooftop.

When she reached the edge, she hit the Zero Gravity button on her spy suit's elbow pad and leaped. The button left her temporarily free of the earth's gravitational pull, and in that split second, she soared through the air to the next store's roof. She landed with a soft thud, made her way to the side, and peered down to the street below.

Her evil uncle, Lubek, walked out of the shadows into a puddle of light cast by a street lamp. The light glinted off a shiny red box tucked under his arm.

"Aha, what have you got there?" Natasha murmured. She put on her super-powered, high-tech, and unbelievably stylish spy glasses and zoomed in on the box.

It can't be, she thought, frowning. She adjusted the focus on her glasses and looked again. *It is! It's a box of chocolates!*

Just then, Lubek disappeared into the shop below her.

Right. Switching to audio! Natasha removed a sophisticated listening device from her utility belt, fastened the ear buds into her ears, and lowered the tiny microphone down the side of the building. Lubek's voice came through, loud and clear.

"Do you have long-stemmed red roses?" he asked. "No other flower store around here does."

Natasha blinked. *Roses?*

"Well, we do," a salesperson replied cheerfully. "We get them and all our plants from a fabulous greenhouse in the next town. Maybe you know it? They have this one plant called the *Oppositus persona.* That's Latin for 'opposite personality.' Anyway, it—"

"I'll take a dozen roses," Lubek interrupted. "Red."

"Certainly, sir." The salesperson sounded offended. "Shall I gift wrap them for you?"

"No, I'll carry them in my teeth," Lubek replied sarcastically.

"Oh, I wouldn't recommend that! Thorns, you know."

"Gah!" Lubek shouted. "Wrap them, imbecile! And put in a card, too: 'For Moira, the sweetest sweet I know.' And have them sent to Moira's Candy Shop on—"

"I know that place! Moira makes the best chocolate. It . . ."

The salesperson's voice trailed off. Natasha imagined Lubek glaring her into silence. She grabbed her Booferberry and hit Oleg's number.

"Boynski here. Who may I say is calling?"

Natasha rolled her eyes. "Oleg, it's Natasha! Lubek is sending roses to a woman named Moira. And he's got a box of chocolates."

Oleg was silent. When he finally spoke, he sounded confused. "Roses and chocolates? Is that code or something?"

"No, it's—hang on." Natasha heard the shop door open. She glanced down at the street. "He's on the move again. I'm—"

Suddenly, a sound like the yowl of an angry cat assaulted her ears. With a grimace of pain, she pulled out the buds. She held one to the

 Booferberry. "Oleg, can you hear that?"

"Ahh!" Oleg cried in reply. "What *is* that?!"

"Lubek is singing a Zoravian love ballad!"

The song ended abruptly and she heard the growl of a motor followed by the slam of a car door. She peeked over the edge. Lubek had just gotten into a cab.

"Gotta go, Oleg! Natasha out."

She reeled in her mini-microphone and stuffed the listening apparatus and her Booferberry back into their holders. Then she swung over the side of the building, slid down a drainpipe, and stepped onto the taxi's back fender just as the cab was pulling away from the curb.

You're not getting away that easily, she thought. She gripped the cab's trunk handle.

Suddenly, the taxi bounced through a large pothole. Natasha lost her hold and landed with a thump on the pavement. By the time she'd jumped to her feet, the cab had disappeared into the night.

"Rats!" She pulled out her Booferberry again. This time, she tapped in her father's number. When his face materialized on the screen, she quickly relayed all she had seen that night.

"Chocolates, roses, and love songs? And he was being nice? Ahhh." Her father smiled knowingly. "It's all clear to me now!"

"Well, it's not clear to me!" Natasha grumbled. "Care to fill me in?"

King Carl's smile broadened. "It's very simple," he said. "Your uncle is in love!"

Chapter Three

Yak Spit

"Lubek . . . is in *love*?" Natasha was so astonished she could barely get the words out.

Her father nodded. "I've seen him act this way once before, back when my father, King Hector, was still on the throne. Lubek was as nasty and conniving then as he is now. Then he fell in love. He showered the lady with gifts of perfume, flowers, and chocolates, serenaded her by moonlight—badly, but still—and even ended his wicked ways."

King Carl sighed. "Unfortunately, it didn't last. My father died around that time, and Lubek took over the kingdom and returned to his old tricks. When the lady discovered his true nature, she ended the relationship."

"How did Lubek handle the breakup?" Natasha asked.

"He collected yak spit."

"Come again?"

Her father made a face. "As you know, Zoravian yaks produce a great deal of drool. Lubek used that drool to ruin romance for everyone in the kingdom. He sprayed it over every flower, drizzled it on every chocolate, and dripped it into every bottle of perfume he could find."

"Gross!" Natasha said.

"To say the least. The only good thing to come out of the whole business was  the peace and quiet we had when he was actually in love." He smiled. "I believe you are experiencing that same peace and quiet now. We must take advantage of it."

Natasha was puzzled. "What do you mean?"

"While Lubek is in love, he will not plot against the kingdom. Therefore, you will not need to spy on him. And so, I think you can pay us a visit."

Natasha caught her breath. "Really, Dad? That would be great!"

"Only for a few days, though, I'm afraid. Should Lubek's relationship end badly—"

"—it could be yak spit all over again,"

Natasha finished.

"Or worse." King Carl stroked his beard thoughtfully. "We need a plan that explains your return to Zoravia. Any ideas?"

Natasha gave a sudden yawn. "Actually, Dad, my brain is feeling a little fried right now!"

"Then go to bed, my dear, and I shall come up with something. Good night."

King Carl vanished from the screen. Natasha made a quick call to Oleg to tell him what she had discovered. She asked him to keep an eye on Moira at the local candy store and then tucked away her Booferberry and hurried back to the O'Briens' house, where she changed into her pajamas, climbed into bed, and fell fast asleep.

She slept in late the next morning. When

she finally went downstairs, she found the O'Brien family, minus Greg, gathered in the kitchen. An elderly man she'd never seen before was there, too.

"Good morning," she said politely. "I'm Natasha."

"Howya." The man jammed a filthy finger up his nose, wiggled it around, and then pulled it out and inspected the gooey morsel stuck on its tip. "I'm KC's grandfather."

"I can see the family resemblance," Natasha said dryly.

"Natasha," Mrs. O'Brien said, "we have a surprise for you!"

Natasha's heart quickened. *Oh, Dad,* she thought, *did you—?*

"We're going to Zoravia!"

"Yes!" Natasha pumped her fist. "That's—"

She paused. "Did you say, *'we're* going to Zoravia'?"

Mrs. O'Brien picked up a slip of paper. "We got this telegram this morning. Listen." She read the telegram aloud. "'You have been randomly selected to take a three-day, all-expenses-paid trip for five to the Turquoise Palace in Zoravia!'" She sighed happily. "I've always wanted to be randomly selected for something!"

"So everyone's going?" Natasha asked.

"Nah, I'm staying here with Cramps!" KC told her.

"With *cramps*?"

"That's his nickname for his grandfather." Mrs. O'Brien ruffled KC's hair affectionately. "But don't worry, that fifth ticket isn't going to waste."

"Why? Who's taking it?"

"Greg," a shrill female voice shrieked from the garage, "be *careful* with that suitcase! It has all my hair accessories in it!"

Mrs. O'Brien beamed and opened the door. A pretty blond girl walked in, trailed by Greg.

Oh, no, Natasha groaned inwardly. *Not Kelly. Anyone but her!*

Chapter Four

Homeward Bound

Natasha retreated upstairs. As she pulled out her suitcase to pack for the trip, she heard her Booferberry.

It was Oleg. "I wanted to wish you a good trip and to reassure you that while you are enjoying your return to our beloved home-land"—his voice broke for a moment—"I will be here. Alone. Keeping an eye on Lubek. Alone."

 "I'm sorry you're not coming, too, Oleg. I'd rather travel with you than Kelly any day!" She sat down on her bed. "In fact, I wish I knew why Dad included the O'Briens at all."

Oleg cleared his throat. "I believe it was so he and your mother could get to know your host family."

"Oh. I guess it would be kind of weird for the king and queen of Zoravia to show up here. Still," she continued, "I was looking forward to being a princess again, even if it is just for a few days. But now I have to be plain old Natasha."

"First off," Oleg said, "there is nothing plain or old about you. Second, you are always a princess, no matter where you are."

"Aw, thanks, Oleg. I—"

"And third," he cut in, "your parents' plan includes you being Princess Natasha while you are home."

"Really? What—"

Just then, Mr. O'Brien knocked on her door to tell her the cab would be there in fifteen minutes to take them to the airport.

"Okay!" she called back. "I better finish packing," she said to Oleg. "I'll bring you back something Zoravian, okay?"

"That would be nice. And I'm sure traveling with Kelly won't be as bad as you imagine."

It wasn't as bad as she imagined. It was much, much worse.

"I've been on this plane for *hours*!" Kelly whined. "I'm going *crazy*!"

She took a sip of her complimentary ginger ale and immediately spat it out. "*Flat!*"

She ate a complimentary peanut instead—

and spat that out, too. "*Rotten!*"

Then she tried to smooth out her skirt. "*Wrinkled!*"

She turned to Greg, who was dozing next to the window. "Are you listening to me?"

"Mmmm," he mumbled. "You're crazy, flat, rotten, and wrinkled."

Suddenly, the plane dipped a wing and started to circle downward.

"Hey, we're beginning our descent!" Natasha said. She looked over Greg's head, hoping to catch a glimpse of the countryside. "Look! It's the Turquoise Palace!"

Kelly glanced out the window. "That's it?" she said disdainfully. "It's so puny!"

Natasha rolled her eyes. "Well, we are thousands of feet above it still."

"And you call that *turquoise*?" Kelly picked up a fashion magazine and flipped through the pages. "Looks more like *aquamarine* to me."

Natasha sat on her hands to keep herself from grabbing the magazine, rolling it up, and swatting Kelly across the nose with it.

Twenty minutes later the plane taxied to the gate. And twenty minutes after that, Natasha saw a beautiful sight—her parents waving to

her at the far end of the ramp.

"It's her!" Greg whispered from behind her.

"Who?" Natasha said, glancing at him. "Queen Lena?"

Greg looked like a lovesick puppy. "No, *her*! Princess Natasha!"

Natasha jerked her head back around. Her eyes widened in shock. Greg was right. Standing there with her parents was. . . *herself*!

"I don't believe it," she gasped.

"Me neither!" Greg moved forward as if in a trance. Then he tripped and landed flat on his face.

Kelly pulled her foot back, stepped over her boyfriend, stuck her nose in

 the air, and walked up the ramp without a backward glance.

Natasha, meanwhile, looked more closely at the princess. So far, her double hadn't done anything but wave and smile.

Just then, Queen Lena shifted slightly. The skirt of her gown swayed toward the princess. But instead of brushing up against Natasha's gown, the queen's dress went *through* it!

Natasha hid a grin. *She's a hologram!*

Chapter Five

The Princess Returns

The Princess Natasha hologram was very convincing from a distance, she had to admit. But she guessed the three-dimensional movie projection wasn't as believable up close because before she and the O'Briens reached the royal family, the hologram walked away.

"Where's she going?" Greg wailed. He started after her.

King Carl stepped in front of him. "She's quite shy and rarely talks to guests, dear boy.

 And as you know, even princesses must heed the call of nature."

Greg looked perplexed. "I didn't hear any call."

"I meant, she's gone to powder her nose."

"Couldn't she do that here?"

"No, no, I mean, she's visiting the water closet."

"Won't the powder get wet?"

King Carl tried one last time. "She's gone to the loo! To the loo!"

"Toodle-oo to you, too!" Greg turned to Natasha. "Your king has a weird way of communicating. By the way, do you see the little boy's room anywhere? I gotta go to the can."

When Greg returned from the restroom, Queen Lena escorted them to the parking garage where two limousines were waiting.

The princess holo-
gram was in the sec-
ond one, still smiling
and waving. Greg
moved eagerly toward
that car.

Queen Lena held
him back with a gentle but firm hand. "Greg,
you, your parents, and your charming girlfriend
will ride in the first car to the Turquoise Palace.
Natasha, please come with us. We're taking
you to your parents' house." She gave her
daughter a sly wink.

Natasha climbed in next to the hologram.
Her parents followed. They sat, tense and
silent, until the first car had pulled away from
the curb. Then they flung their arms around
one another in a group hug.

"This hologram is amazing," Natasha said
when they finally broke apart. "Still, I can't

believe no one noticed how much she and I look alike."

Queen Lena pushed a button and the hologram disappeared. "I'm sure if we pointed it out, they would. But remember, the O'Briens believe you are a simple exchange student on her way to visit her parents. It would be quite a stretch for them to suddenly see you as the princess."

She pulled a sparkling tiara and silk gown from a box beneath her seat. "Of course, that doesn't mean you can't be the princess, at least for a few days!"

Natasha glowed with happiness. "I can handle that!"

When she emerged from the limousine at the Turquoise Palace, she was dressed from head to toe in royal finery. Greg's eyes bugged out when he saw her. Kelly, on the other hand, turned up her nose.

"You call that a gown?" she said. "More like a sack. And I've seen bigger jewels on...on...on other kinds of jewelry."

"Come!" Queen Lena beckoned them all inside. "Dinner is waiting."

At the table, Greg rested his chin in his hand and stared at Natasha dreamily. "You are soooo—*Ow!*"

"Sorry, my fork slipped," Kelly said, pulling her utensil from his arm and setting it down next to her plate.

After dinner, the queen showed the visitors around the moonlit gardens. King Carl, meanwhile, drew Natasha aside. "It is so good to see you, my dear."

Natasha smiled. "You, too, Dad. I—"

"You've got an alert!"

Her smile faded. "Was that what I think it was?"

King Carl pulled his Booferberry from his robe pocket and hit the receive button. Oleg appeared on the screen.

"Your Majesty, Princess Natasha, I have terrible news! Lubek has lost his love!"

Oleg quickly relayed what had happened. "I followed him to his lady friend's candy store. He had the chocolates. He went in. Seven and a half minutes passed. Then the door burst open wide, and the candy was thrown out as well as the roses he'd sent earlier. I heard a woman yell, 'How dare you buy chocolates from another store?' Then Lubek, his face like thunder, stormed off into the night. I tried to tail him but he was too swift. And now I can't find him."

King Carl heaved a great sigh. "Oleg, you are a good spy, one of Zoravia's best. But even if you did know where Lubek had gone off to, you would not be able to stop him by yourself." He turned a sad eye to his daughter.

Natasha slowly pulled the tiara from her hair. "Looks like I'm trading in my princess dress for my spy suit. Fire up the supersonic jet and come get me, Oleg."

Chapter Six

Bye for Now

Later that night, Natasha was back in her regular clothes and standing on the roof of the palace's highest tower with her father. She scanned the night sky. Suddenly, she saw a pinpoint of green light that grew steadily larger and brighter.

"There's Oleg," she said. She hugged King Carl tightly as Oleg's jet got into position above her.

"Good luck, my dear girl," her father said. "And Natasha, do your best to return in time to fly home with the O'Briens!"

Nodding, Natasha grabbed the rope ladder Oleg had dropped down. She climbed up and into the plane. Once she was inside, the plane soared back into the sky. She watched her father and the Turquoise Palace  fade away and then hurried up to the cockpit.

"Hi, Oleg," she said, flopping into the seat next to her partner. "Want me to fly for a while?"

He glanced at her. "No, you sleep," he replied. "I'll wake you when we reach Illinois."

Natasha took him up on the offer. She awoke when the plane was setting down in the small Fountain Park airport.

"I'm going to the O'Briens' to get my spy

gear," she told Oleg. "I'll check the Lubek Locator, see if I can find him with that. I'll call you with the results."

As Natasha made her way across town toward the O'Briens' house, she thought about the situation. By her calculations, Lubek had been in a love-lost rage for more than twelve hours—plenty of time for him to put together a thoroughly evil plot.

She reached the house, climbed the tree to

her bedroom window, and slipped inside.

A horrific smell hit her the moment her feet

touched the floor. She opened her bedroom door a crack. The smell was even worse in the main house. She ran into the hallway, peered down the stairs, and smothered a gasp.

The house was completely trashed. Crushed potato chips littered the steps. Wet towels hung from the banister. A balled-up sock sat in a puddle of yogurt—or curdled milk—she  wasn't sure which, but knew she didn't want to find out. At the bottom of the stairs was a teetering tower of empty cans. *Baked beans*, the labels on the cans read.

"Aren't those beans hot yet, Cramps?" she heard KC yell from below. "I'm starving!" Then she heard a sound like a balloon with a slow leak. "'Scuse me. Again."

Well, that explains the smell, she thought, waving her hand under her nose and retreating back to her bedroom.

There, she quickly changed into her spy suit, clipped her utility belt and gadgets into place, and flicked on her Lubek Locator, a handheld  computer programmed to identify the whereabouts of anything resembling her uncle. Even though the Locator wasn't one hundred percent accurate, it was the best way to start looking for him.

She instructed the device to scan the whole town. Nothing. She widened the scope of her search. This time, she got a hit: a flashing orange dot appeared in the next town. She zeroed in on the dot.

Lubek, it turned out, was in the greenhouse the flower shop salesperson had mentioned.

She thought of calling Oleg for a lift, but decided to borrow KC's motorized scooter.

Helmet and spy glasses in place, she drove to the next town, parked the scooter a block away from the green-  house, and covered the remaining ground silently on foot. It was dark out, but she had no trouble finding the building, a large glass structure dimly lit by special plant-growing lightbulbs. Lubek was inside the greenhouse, just as the Locator had indicated.

Okay, now let's see what you're up to! She adjusted her spy glasses and settled under a tree to watch her uncle.

Chapter Seven

Greenhouse Effect

Lubek bent over a potted plant and poked a long needle into one of its large, cuplike leaves. Suddenly, the leaf snapped shut around the needle—and one of Lubek's fingers. His face contorted with pain but he didn't pull free.

The leaf slowly opened. Lubek removed the needle, along with an oozing glob

of sap. He deposited the glob into a container filled with similar globs and moved on to the next leaf.

Well, it's not yak saliva, Natasha thought, *but it looks just as disgusting.*

She touched a button on the frames of her glasses. The lenses zoomed in on a label attached to the plant's pot.

Oppositus persona, the label read. *An extremely rare carnivorous plant, its sap can cause temporary changes in personality. The sap was once used in sacred rituals, but use of it is now banned.*

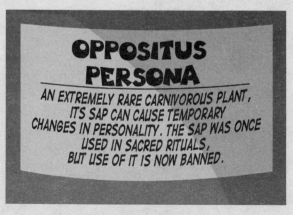

OPPOSITUS PERSONA

AN EXTREMELY RARE CARNIVOROUS PLANT, ITS SAP CAN CAUSE TEMPORARY CHANGES IN PERSONALITY. THE SAP WAS ONCE USED IN SACRED RITUALS, BUT USE OF IT IS NOW BANNED.

Natasha removed her glasses. *Okay, now I know what that goop is and what it does. But it still doesn't tell me what he plans to do with it.*

She took out her listening device, using suction cups to attach the mini-microphone to the nearest glass pane, and put the buds in her ears.

"Valentine's Day! Romance! Gah!" Lubek muttered. "I hate love."

He pulled another glob of sap from the plant and put it in the container. Then he gave an evil laugh. "That's the last of it! Now I can finish putting my plan into action." He held the container up high. "With this, I can make everyone who is in love suddenly discover they

can't stand the person they're in love with!"
He threw his head back and laughed again.

Of all the rotten . . . I've heard enough!
Natasha stowed away her listening gear, and
then rushed to the greenhouse door and
yanked it open.

"Leave that leaf alone, Lubek!" she cried.

Lubek spun around. His face contorted with

anger. "You! You dare to interfere with me—
and use my name in a sentence riddled with
alliteration?!"

"Yes—and yes! Now put down that needle
and step away from the sap."

"Never!" He picked up his container.

She struck a fighting stance. "Then you leave me no choice but to—hey! Stop!"

Too late, she noticed that the greenhouse had a back door. By the time she'd crossed to the exit, he had slammed the door shut after him. Then she heard the rasp of a key in a lock. Lubek had locked her in!

She dashed to the front door. But Lubek had beaten her there and turned the key in that lock, too. He smiled at her maliciously and dangled the key where she could see it. Then he turned and vanished into the night.

Natasha whirled around, searching for another way out. She struck her head with her hand. "Well, duh! The walls are made of glass! I can just break my way out."

She picked up an empty flowerpot and pre-pared to heave it at the nearest wall. Then she hesitated.

These are tropical plants. If I break the glass, the cold air could kill them.

She put down the pot and examined the front door instead. Unlike the walls, it was made of metal. The doorknob was metal, too. She knelt down to look at the knob more close-ly. To her delight, she saw that it was held in place with two screws. If she could remove those screws, she could remove the doorknob and get at the lock.

With a grin, she opened the tool kit on her utility belt and took out a battery-operated screwdriver. She stuck the tip into the screw and pressed a button. The screw backed out and fell to the floor at her feet. One minute later, the other screw had joined the first. The knob dropped into her hand. She felt inside the

hole, found the lock mechanism, and tripped it.
One push on the door, and she was free!

Chapter Eight

The Wrath of Oleg

As she sprinted back to the scooter, she dialed Oleg on the Booferberry. When he answered, his voice sounded strangely thick.

"Oleg, are you eating something?"

"Just a piece of chocolate," he answered. "After I dropped you off, I went by Moira's Candy Shop to see if Lubek was there. The shop was closed so I sneaked around back to see if he was in the warehouse. That's when I got lucky."

"Lubek was in the warehouse?"

"No, boxes of chocolate were in the warehouse!"

"And so you just took some?"

"Only two! And I left some money on a table there," he said defensively.

"Well, if you're done satisfying your sweet tooth—"

"I've only had one piece!"

"Just eat and listen at the same time, okay?" She quickly told him all that had happened at the greenhouse. "I'm heading to your place. Meantime, I need you to find out all you can about that *Oppositus persona* plant and its sap." She heard a crinkling sound and rolled her eyes. "You *can* eat and do research at the same time, can't you? Natasha out."

As she buzzed back to town on KC's scooter, she thought about Lubek, his lost loves, and the sap.

The last time he was dumped he ruined flowers, perfume, and candy. Flowers, perfume, and candy are everywhere right now because of Valentine's Day. If he can somehow get the sap onto or into one of those things, he could turn lots of people who love each other into lots of people who hate each other. And even though the sap's effects are temporary, that kind of hatred could leave lasting damage!

She arrived at Oleg's building. "What have you found out?" she called as she burst through his door.

Oleg was seated at his computer. He stiffened at the sound of her voice. Then he slowly swung around and faced her.

"Do you make it a habit to enter without knocking?" he snarled.

Her eyes widened at the unexpected anger in his voice. She took a step back.

"Are—are you okay?"

"I'd be better if you weren't around!" He stood up abruptly. His chair rolled backward. Its wheels crackled over a litter of dark brown paper wrappers and then bumped to a stop against an empty candy box marked *Sweet Nothings*.

Natasha stared at the box. "Oleg," she said, her mind whirling, "did you eat that entire box of chocolates since I last talked to you?"

"None of your business, Miss Nosey-Boots!"

She looked around the room and spied a second box of Sweet Nothings. She started toward it.

Oleg snatched it up before she reached it. "Get your own box!"

She held up her hands in surrender. "I think you should know something about that candy."

"Oh yeah? What?"

"I believe Lubek has somehow added *Oppositus persona* sap to it!"

"Yeah, right! If that were true, then I would be feeling the exact opposite of everything I normally feel!"

She raised an eyebrow and waited.

A look of understanding crossed Oleg's face, battled with the rage already there—and, fortunately, won. "I hate you," he said wonderingly.

"I mean, I really, *really* hate you!"

"The sap's effects are temporary, so you'll get over it," she assured him. "Meanwhile, can you help me?"

"I'd rather not," he replied.

"Then you leave me no choice." She took a deep breath and kicked his computer monitor with all her might. The screen shattered with a shower of sparks.

"Hey!" Oleg's eyes turned dark. His chest heaved. His hands balled into fists.

Then slowly his fury ebbed. He turned to

Natasha with a broad smile. "You have reversed the effects of the sap by doing something to make me hate you!"

"You're very smart, Oleg!"

His face clouded over.

"I mean, took you long enough to figure it out, you dimwit!"

She pulled out her Lubek Locator and searched for her uncle. She found him right where she expected him to be—in the warehouse attached to the sweetshop where Oleg had "purchased" his chocolates.

"Come on, you idiot," she said to her partner, "we've got to stop Lubek before he turns more friends into enemies!"

Chapter Nine

The Sap Gets Zapped

Natasha insulted Oleg the whole way to the shop. "I don't know how Kelly does it," she said finally. "Coming up with mean things to say to people is totally exhausting!"

Thinking of Kelly reminded her that she needed to be back in Zoravia in time to fly home with the O'Briens.

I can't worry about that now, she thought. *Not when there's chocolate to destroy!*

When they reached Moira's Candy Shop,

Natasha peered inside. To her relief, she didn't see any boxes of Sweet Nothings. She guessed that meant the sap-tainted candy wasn't in the store. Not yet, anyway.

She and Oleg crept up to the warehouse's main door, sneaked inside, and hid behind a stack of crates.

Lubek was hunched over a table, stirring something. He poured the mixture into a spray bottle. Then he picked up a box of Sweet Nothings, peeled off the plastic wrap, lifted the lid, and covered the choco-lates with a fine mist from the bottle.

"Rewrap this and add it to the stack!" Lubek barked.

"Yes, sir!"

Natasha and Oleg jumped. Neither of them had seen Lubek's henchman lurking in the shadows. They exchanged a worried glance. *Were there any more about?*

There's one way to find out, Natasha thought. As Lubek opened another box of chocolates, she leaped from their hiding place, ran across the floor to his table, and snatched up the spray bottle.

"Ha!" she cried. "Now what are you going to do?"

"This!" With a lightning-quick movement, Lubek picked up a chocolate and threw it at

her. She ducked just before it struck her. The next sweet, however, hit her on the shoulder. It burst on impact, showering her with sticky goo.

Still clutching the bottle, she sprinted back to the crates.

"Get her!" Lubek roared.

His henchman charged after her. *"Yeee-aaahhhh!"* he bellowed.

She sprayed sap mixture into his open mouth. He gulped in surprise and then froze, dropped his arms, and gave her a dazed smile.

"You're pretty," he said.

"Oh, brother," Natasha muttered. "Come on, Oleg, let's get out of here."

"Why should I listen to you?" Oleg said, crossing his

arms over his chest.

The henchman smiled at Oleg. "Isn't she pretty?"

Oleg narrowed his eyes. "She's *irritating.*"

"I think she's pretty."

"She's hideous and irritating and bossy!"

"What's taking you so long?!" Lubek shouted.

Now it was the henchman's turn to narrow his eyes. "That's the one who's hideous and irritating and bossy. And I'm not going to take it anymore."

He charged out from behind the crates, tackled Lubek to the ground, and sat on him.

"Gah! Get off me, you worthless lump!"

Natasha darted forward and zapped Lubek in the mouth with the sap.

Lubek relaxed and

smiled up at his henchman. "You're pretty."

"Well, that was easy," Natasha said. "Now come on, Oleg, we—"

Oleg glowered at her.

"I mean, *I* have to destroy those chocolates. And I absolutely do not want your help!"

"Oh, I'm helping you, all right!" Oleg cried. "You can't tell me what not to do!" He opened a box of Sweet Nothings, threw the chocolates to the ground, and stomped on them. "Ha! What do you think of that?"

"I think it's awful!" Natasha said. "And I hope you stop!"

Oleg smiled triumphantly and reached for another  box. Twenty minutes later, there wasn't a Sweet Nothing that didn't have his shoe print on it.

Chapter Ten

Home Sweet Home

When Oleg was done destroying the chocolates, Natasha filled two buckets with soapy water and found some sponges. She handed the buckets and sponges to Lubek and his henchman. "Clean up this mess, will you?"

"Sure, pretty girl!" they both cooed.

While they scrubbed, she dumped the remaining sap mixture into a potted plant. *Back to nature!* she thought. When the warehouse was clean, she used the wire from her grappling hook to tie up Lubek and his henchman.

"Thank you, pretty girl!" they said.

"You're welcome, nasty men!"

Natasha and Oleg raced back to his place so he could get the keys to the supersonic jet. His second box of Sweet Nothings was still on his table. Natasha tucked it into her spy suit so that Oleg wouldn't be tempted to eat them.

They made another stop at the O'Briens' house. Natasha sneaked into her bedroom and changed her clothes. Then she sniffed the foul air.

I can't let the O'Briens come home to this, she thought. She tiptoed downstairs and left six Sweet Nothings on the kitchen table for KC and Cramps to find.

Hours later, the supersonic jet was hovering over the Turquoise Palace. Natasha had called ahead to let her parents know that all was well and that she was returning. The king and queen were waiting for her on the rooftop.

She embraced them tightly. "How have things been here?"

Queen Lena sighed. "Greg follows the hologram around everywhere. Kelly injures Greg whenever possible. Your host parents

are suffering from upset stomach after eating too many boofer fruits. Other than that, it has been a delightful visit."

The next morning, King Carl and Queen Lena drove the O'Briens, Natasha, and Kelly back to the airport.

"Good-bye and thank you for your wonderful hospitality!" Mr. and Mrs. O'Brien called.

"Look at how the princess is waving and smiling at me!" Greg whispered to Natasha.

Natasha pulled the half-empty box of Sweet Nothings from her backpack. "Say, care for a chocolate?"

"Okay." Greg ate one. His dreamy expression turned sour.

"You know, I never noticed it before, but there's something really transparent about that princess." He boarded the plane without a backward glance at the hologram.

"I am *so* not sitting next to him on the way

home," Kelly growled.

"Care for a chocolate?" Natasha asked.

Kelly ate one. Her sour expression turned dreamy. She found Greg's hand and held it lovingly.

"Drop dead!" Greg yanked his hand free. Kelly just smiled.

Eight hours later, the taxi deposited the family and their luggage in the O'Briens' driveway.

Mrs. O'Brien was the first one in the door. "KC! Cramps! *What have you two done to my house?*"

Natasha's heart sank. Apparently the chocolates hadn't worked. Then she stepped inside and gasped.

The whole house was spotless. It smelled, not of bean-induced flatulence, but of fresh-baked cinnamon rolls. Unbelievably, KC and Cramps were clean, too. And neither of them had so much as a pinky in his nose.

Up in her room, Natasha pulled the empty Sweet Nothings box from her suitcase. She wondered how much longer the sap's effects would linger.

Just then, strains of music floated up from below.

"Kel-ly, la la la la . . . Kel-ly, tra la la la. . ."

"Oh, Greggy," Kelly trilled, "this video is just the. . . the . . ." Her voice trailed away. When she spoke again, she sounded like her old self. "Just the *worst* Valentine's Day present ever!"

Natasha heard laughter coming from outside. She looked down and saw KC and Cramps flinging muddy slushballs at each other.

Guess everyone's back to normal, she thought.

"You've got an alert!"

Including Lubek! She flicked on her

Booferberry and greeted her parents.

"Hi, Mom and Dad! Let me guess . . . Lubek's at it again. Well, don't you worry."

She struck a fighting stance.

"Princess Natasha is ready for her next assignment!"